KATHRYN LASKY
THE LIBRARIAN WHO MEASURED THE EARTH

ILLUSTRATED BY KEVIN HAWKES

Little, Brown and Company
Boston   New York   Toronto   London

To all children who dare to
ask questions and continue to wonder
—K. L.

To David, who is never satisfied
—K. H.

First Edition

Library of Congress Cataloging-in-Publication Data

Lasky, Kathryn.
    The librarian who measured the earth / Kathryn Lasky ;
illustrated by Kevin Hawkes. — 1st ed.
        p.   cm.
    Summary: Describes the life and work of Eratosthenes, the Greek
geographer and astronomer who accurately measured the circumference
of the earth.
    ISBN 0-316-51526-4
    1. Eratosthenes — Juvenile literature. 2. Earth — Figure —
Measurement — Juvenile literature. 3. Astronomy, Greek — Juvenile
literature. 4. Geography, Ancient — Juvenile literature.
5. Geographers — Greece — Biography — Juvenile literature.
6. Astronomers — Greece — Biography — Juvenile literature.
[1. Eratosthenes. 2. Geographers. 3. Earth.] I. Hawkes, Kevin,
ill. II. Title.
QB36.E73L37   1994
520' .92 — dc20
[B]   92-42656

10 9 8 7 6

SC

Published simultaneously in Canada
by Little, Brown & Company (Canada) Limited

Paintings done in acrylics on two-ply museum board. Color separations
made by South China Printing Company (1988) Limited. Text set in Palatino by
Typographic House and display lines set in Pericles.
Printed and bound by South China Printing Company (1988) Limited.

Printed in Hong Kong

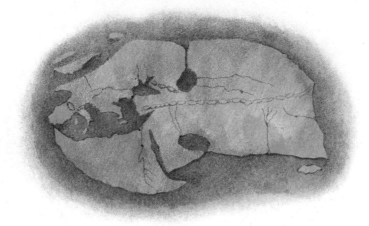

AUTHOR'S NOTE

I became interested in the life of Eratosthenes and his contributions to our present-day knowledge of the earth when my husband, Christopher Knight, was editing *Higher Than Everest*, a film for the public television series *Nova* that explained techniques for measuring mountains and surveying the earth. Most of the methods were high-tech, involving strategies such as satellite imaging and global positioning systems. Leafing through his research notes, I was fascinated to come upon the name of Eratosthenes. Eratosthenes' methods for determining the circumference of the earth involved camels, plumb lines, and measuring the angles of shadows. Crude? Homemade? Perhaps. Yet his measurement for the circumference of the earth was within two hundred miles of the measurements made with the help of modern technology within the last five years! I wanted to find out more about this man who lived over two thousand years ago.

It may seem odd that a man who gave us many answers left so many questions about himself. For indeed Eratosthenes remains a mystery to us. Despite all the volumes he wrote, he left behind no personal documents, no diaries, no birth records. Much, of course, has been written about the period. Classical historians and historians of science know a great deal about the time in which Eratosthenes lived and have scraped together bits and pieces about him, particularly during his years as chief librarian at the great library in Alexandria, Egypt.

There is much that we do not know nor ever will for sure. Such gaps exist in all histories. We cannot fill them in by making up facts, but we can try to responsibly imagine based on what we already know, which is what I've tried to do in this book. This is not an uncommon way for historians to work. To delve into a life of a remarkable man like Eratosthenes is a challenge of the most joyful sort, for his curiosity about life is contagious. If I could not have lived two thousand years ago and been one of his students or a reader at the great library in Alexandria, the next best thing is to write a book about such a man.

More than two thousand years ago, a very smart baby was born. His name was Eratosthenes (AIR-uh-TOS-thuh-neez). His parents were Greek, and they lived in Cyrene (SĪ-ree-nee), a Greek city on the coast of Africa in the country that is now called Libya.

Even as a baby, Eratosthenes was curious and full of wonder.

He would crawl across the kitchen floor to follow the path of ants.

He wondered why there were beads of water on the cistern in the morning.

And in the evening, when he looked out the window of his bedroom, he wondered why the stars stayed in the sky.

When he could speak, he began asking hundreds and even thousands of questions:

How far away is the sun?

What is it made of?

Where do the winds come from?

What makes the stars move?

Many of these questions his parents couldn't answer.

When he was six years old, he went to school. It was called the gymnasium. Although the original meaning of the word was exercise ground, a gymnasium was also a school. Every morning, Eratosthenes, like other Greek boys, would be taken there by a family slave.

At the gymnasium there were no desks, no paper, and no pencils. And there were no girls. The girls stayed home and learned to cook and weave. Not many learned to read or write.

Students sat on the floor, and instead of pens they had styluses, sticks with one sharp end that were used for writing on tablets made of wax.

Eratosthenes loved the gymnasium. It was a chance to ask more questions.

In between asking questions, he and the other students learned reading, writing, arithmetic, music, and poetry. They even learned how to play the lyre and recite poetry at the same time.

Eratosthenes was good at all these subjects, and he was a real whiz in math. But his absolute favorite subject was geography. He bombarded his teachers with questions:

How much of the earth is land?

How high is the highest mountain?

Is there a map of the earth?

When Eratosthenes had learned all he could at the gymnasium, he, like many Greek boys, was sent to the famous Greek capital city to learn more. He said good-bye to his parents and his teachers and sailed to Athens.

In Athens he studied mathematics, philosophy, and science. There wasn't much time for the lyre or marbles, but there was always time for questions.

In addition to being a great questioner, Eratosthenes was a terrific list maker. He liked making lists. It was a good way to organize information so it could be shared with other people. He made a list of all the important dates in the history of Greece. This kind of list is called a chronology. He also made a list of all the winners of the Olympic Games. And he began to write books. He wrote one on comedy, one on history, and one on the constellations.

Eratosthenes' name started to get around.

When Eratosthenes was thirty years old, a king called Ptolemy III, the ruler of Egypt, asked him to serve as tutor for his son Philopator in Alexandria. Eratosthenes was ecstatic. For a scholar like himself, Alexandria was the most exciting place to be. It was the center of all learning. It boasted a library and a museum that were the best in the world. All the great questions about science, literature, and history could be asked and researched here.

For indeed this museum was not just a collection of things on exhibit. The word *museum* literally means place of the Muses. In Greek mythology, the Muses are the nine daughters of Zeus, who help inspire artists and scientists.

At the museum there were laboratories and libraries, dining halls and private studios. There were special promenades that wound through quiet gardens for thoughtful strolls. Great minds were supposed to come to this place to read, study, and be inspired. And if the stomachs of these great minds started to growl with hunger, there were meals—porridge, fruit, nuts, and cheese.

It was here that the first dictionaries and encyclopedias were written. It was in the dissecting laboratories of the museum that a scientist named Herophilius first recognized the connection between a person's heartbeat and pulse and discovered the differences between arteries and veins.

A man named Ctesibius invented the first water-driven clock
as well as the first keyboard musical instrument.

It was at the Alexandria Museum that punctuation and grammar were invented by Aristophanes. Before this, one word ran into the next with no spaces between them. There were no question marks, periods, or exclamation points either. Reading was hard!

And two thousand years ago, books were handwritten on scrolls of animal skins or papyrus, paper made from a tall grass that grows along the Nile. In the library at Alexandria, there were seven hundred thousand papyrus scrolls and forty librarians who, just like modern-day librarians, helped readers find what they were looking for and kept the materials in order. Each scroll was rolled up on a painted stick and tied with a colored string with a name tag attached. Often the scrolls were tucked into clay jars or simply placed on wooden shelves. There was a lot of rolling and tagging and tying that had to be done to keep a library as large as the one at Alexandria in order.

Eratosthenes fit right in with all his questions and ideas. In fact he got a new nickname, Pentathlos. The word refers to an athlete who competes in five different events. It had also come to mean all-rounder in Greek. They called him that because he was good at so many different things.

It was not long after he arrived that the head librarian died and Eratosthenes was appointed in his place. For a question asker and a list maker like Eratosthenes, being the head librarian was a dream come true. Now he could start to find answers to all of his questions. And the questions that were beginning to interest him the most were the ones right under his own two feet: questions about the earth—geography.

As chief librarian, Eratosthenes was kept busy helping other scholars find information. He also had to keep in the good graces of his employer, King Ptolemy, who had a touchy and nervous temperament. In fact, a royal flatterer was employed just to keep the king's spirits up. But Eratosthenes himself had to be ready with compliments and praise for the king at all times.

So on one occasion, when he had solved a particularly difficult geometry problem, Eratosthenes dedicated the solution to the king. He then wrote a little poem about it and had it carved into a column that he had erected in the king's honor.

Eratosthenes' main interest, however, was not writing poetry to flatter the king. It was geography.

Once upon a time it had been thought that the earth was flat. Then for a while people thought that it was the shape of a cylinder. But by the time Eratosthenes was born, they knew for sure that the earth was round, a sphere. They had known this for at least one hundred years. But Eratosthenes had a lot of other questions about the earth. How far does the earth tilt on its axis? Does the ocean go all the way around the earth? One of the most interesting questions of all was how big around *was* the earth? It seemed impossible to figure out, for one could not walk around the earth without running into an ocean, and at that time the Greeks did not have ships that they would dare sail as far as these oceans might reach. Could one, however, stand in one spot and figure it out?

Eratosthenes began his research, unrolling scroll upon scroll, looking for bits and pieces of information that would help him answer his questions. He soon realized that the information he was looking for was scattered all over the place — in math scrolls, scrolls about people, and scrolls about history. In the richest library on earth, there was no single scroll that combined even a few of the answers. For someone like Eratosthenes, who liked to organize information, it was clear that before he could find any answers, the facts must be brought together and rolled up in one single scroll.

Eratosthenes knew what he must do. He had to write the first complete geography book.

It would take Eratosthenes many years. Much of the information about the earth that Eratosthenes wanted to include was mathematical and could never be found in scrolls or by talking to people from other lands. Eratosthenes had to figure out methods of knowing, of measuring, of describing. And, more than anything, he wanted to measure the circumference of the earth. He knew his book would be incomplete without it.

Nobody had ever thought of measuring the size of such a large circle as the circumference of the earth — nobody except for Eratosthenes. Perhaps he imagined the earth as a grapefruit. If it is sliced in half, you can see its sections. In order to measure the distance all the way around the edge of the grapefruit (the circumference), you would need to know only the distance along the edge of one section (the arc) and how many of these same-size sections it would take to make up the whole grapefruit.

How could Eratosthenes find out how many sections were needed? He knew that every circle, whether it is as small as a grapefruit or as big as the earth, is made up of 360 degrees. So if he could measure the inside angle of one section of his imaginary grapefruit in degrees, he could divide 360 by that number and know how many sections of that size would make up the whole.

Eratosthenes pictured a section of the earth whose outside edge
ran from Alexandria to Syene (SĪ-ee-nee), a city in southern Egypt.
If he could figure out the distance between Alexandria and Syene,
and if he could measure the inside angle of the section they
created, he would be able to calculate the earth's circumference.
But how would he ever be able to measure that angle? It lay far
below the ground, at the center of the earth.

Eratosthenes realized that the sun could help him with his angle
problem, and he picked Syene for a reason. He had heard from a
caravan passing through Alexandria that on the twenty-first day
of June at precisely midday, the sun would shine directly down a
certain well in Syene, lighting up the well but casting no shadows
on its walls. But at the exact same time in Alexandria, shadows
would be cast.

Eratosthenes knew why. It was because the earth was round. If the earth were flat, the sun would strike every place at the same angle and the shadows would all be exactly the same.

Eratosthenes knew a thing or two about shadows and angles. He knew you could measure the angle of the sun by the shadow it cast. And he knew, from the mathematical texts he had read, that the angle of the sun in Alexandria at noon on June 21 would be the same as the angle that lay at the center of the earth making the inside of his Alexandria-to-Syene "grapefruit" section.

So Eratosthenes walked out of the library a few minutes before noon on the twenty-first day of June to measure a midday shadow at Alexandria, just as the sun was falling straight down the well at Syene. He measured an angle of about 7.2 degrees. Then he divided 360 by 7.2, which equals 50. Now he knew that it would take 50 Alexandria-to-Syene sections to make up the circumference of the earth.

But knowing that was still not enough. Eratosthenes had to know the length of his section's arc — the distance between the two cities. Then he could multiply this distance by 50 to find the distance around the whole earth. It would be so simple!

But it wasn't. There was a problem. The problem was camels! Camels were the main manner of transport in the desert, and Eratosthenes had planned to measure the distance between the two cities by calculating how long it took camels to get from one city to another. He thought camels would be perfect. But he forgot that they are ornery, stubborn, and have minds of their own.

Some camel caravans went slow and some went fast and some camels ran off in the wrong direction. No matter how hard Eratosthenes tried, he could not record travel times for camels that were accurate enough for his mathematical equations.

Finally he threw up his hands in despair. "Enough with these camels. I'm going to see the king!"

He asked the king if he could borrow the services of his best bematists — surveyors trained to walk with equal steps. In this way linear distances could be measured with some accuracy.

The king agreed. And the bematists he supplied walked with equal steps just as they had been trained to do. It was then easy to estimate that the distance between Alexandria and Syene was five thousand stades. A stade was supposed to equal the length of a Greek stadium. The stade that Eratosthenes used was 515 feet, or just under one-tenth of a mile.

Eratosthenes now had all the numbers he needed for the formula. He calculated the circumference of the earth to be 252,000 stades, or 24,662 miles. When the earth was remeasured in this century, there was only a two-hundred-mile difference between the modern-day figure and the one that Eratosthenes had calculated over two thousand years ago!

Eratosthenes' measurements provided the first accurate, mathematically based map of the world. His *Geographica*, the first geography book of the world, was now complete.

Eratosthenes lived to be a very old man. He continued to work on math problems and to study and measure the earth. But most important of all, he kept asking questions.

No question was ever too big or small for Eratosthenes to think about.

AFTERWORD

Two thousand years before Columbus sailed to the New World, people knew for sure that the earth was round. As long ago as 450 B.C., a Greek scholar named Philoaus and others became convinced of this because of the changing positions of stars in the sky, the way ships disappeared as they moved farther from the coast toward a horizon, and the shadows of the earth that appeared during eclipses of the moon. By the time of Aristotle, scholars agreed that the earth was a sphere — but how big a sphere remained a mystery. That mystery was solved by Eratosthenes. There is no doubt that Eratosthenes was a genius. Like all great thinkers, the success of his work depended on those who came before him.

Mathematics was highly developed by the third century B.C., when Eratosthenes was alive. Ratio tables, which were part of Eratosthenes' calculations of the angles such as those formed by the shadows at Alexandria and Syene, were well established by Babylonian times. There was even a formula for measuring the circumference of a circle, but Eratosthenes did not use this particular one. He made up his own. Greeks had long studied geometry. They knew that when lines were drawn through a circle certain angles always matched. This was an important geometric truth that allowed Eratosthenes to calculate how many pieces of the "grapefruit" there were, thereby calculating the circumference of the actual earth.

When Columbus finally did set out to sail west from Spain to the Indies, he should have paid more attention to Eratosthenes' calculations. Instead he looked at maps done by Greek geographers after Eratosthenes. These geographers made some serious mistakes and showed an earth that was not so big around. Columbus thought it would be a quick trip to the Indies. He was wrong. But perhaps if he had believed Eratosthenes' measurements, in which the oceans of the world looked so huge and the distances between land so far, he would have never even tried!

All knowledge builds on existing knowledge. But it takes the curiosity and inspiration of a man like Eratosthenes to figure out how to use that knowledge to answer old questions and create new ones that will alter civilization and our view of the world for years to come.

BIBLIOGRAPHY

Kathryn Lasky:

Asimov, Isaac. *How Did We Find Out the Earth Is Round?* New York: Walker & Co., 1972.

Boorstin, Daniel J. *The Discoverers: A History of Man's Search to Know His World and Himself.* New York: Random House, 1983.

Burton, Harry E. *The Discovery of the Ancient World.* Cambridge, Mass.: Harvard University Press, 1932.

Daly, Charles P. *The Early History of Cartography.* New York, 1879.

Hathaway, George. *The Story of Maps and Mapmaking.* New York: Golden Press, 1966.

Jones, David E. H. "The Great Museum at Alexandria: Its Ascent to Glory." *Smithsonian* (December 1971 and January 1972).

Morison, Samuel Eliot. *Admiral of the Ocean Sea: A Life of Christopher Columbus.* Boston: Little, Brown, 1941.

Muhly, James D. "Ancient Cartography." *Expedition* 20 (Winter 1978).

Sarton, George. "Geography and Chronology in the Third Century: Eratosthenēs of Cyrēnē." Chap. 6 in *A History of Science.* Cambridge, Mass.: Harvard University Press, 1959.

Kevin Hawkes:

Benevolo, Leonardo. *The History of the City.* London: Scolar Press, 1980.

Boardman, John, Jasper Griffin, and Oswyn Murray, eds. *Greece and the Hellenistic World.* Oxford History of the Classical World. Oxford: Oxford University Press, 1991.

Bowman, Alan K. *Egypt After the Pharoahs: 332 B.C.–A.D. 642.* Berkeley and Los Angeles: University of California Press, 1986.

Camp, John M. *The Athenian Agora: Excavations in the Heart of Classical Athens.* London: Thames and Hudson, 1986.

Fox, Robin L. *The Search for Alexander.* Boston: Little, Brown, 1980.

Grant, Neil. *The Greeks: How They Lived.* New York: Mallard Press, 1990.

Holloway, R. Ross. *A View of Greek Art.* Providence: Brown University Press, 1973.

Marrou, Henri I. *A History of Education in Antiquity.* New York: Sheed and Ward, 1956.

Pearson, Anne. *Ancient Greece* (Eyewitness Books). New York: Knopf, 1992.

Pollitt, J. J. *Art in the Hellenistic Age.* Cambridge, England: Cambridge University Press, 1986.

Richter, Gisela M. A. *The Metropolitan Museum of Art Handbook of the Greek Collection.* Cambridge, Mass.: Harvard University Press, 1953.

Rodgers, Williams L. *Greek and Roman Naval Warfare.* Annapolis: United States Naval Institute, 1964.

Sachs, Curt. *The History of Musical Instruments.* New York: Norton, 1940.

Sansone, David. *Greek Athletics and the Genesis of Sport.* Berkeley and Los Angeles: University of California Press, 1988.

Welch, Kenneth F. *The History of Clocks and Watches.* New York: Drake, 1972.

Wycherley, R. E. *How the Greeks Built Cities.* New York: Norton, 1962.

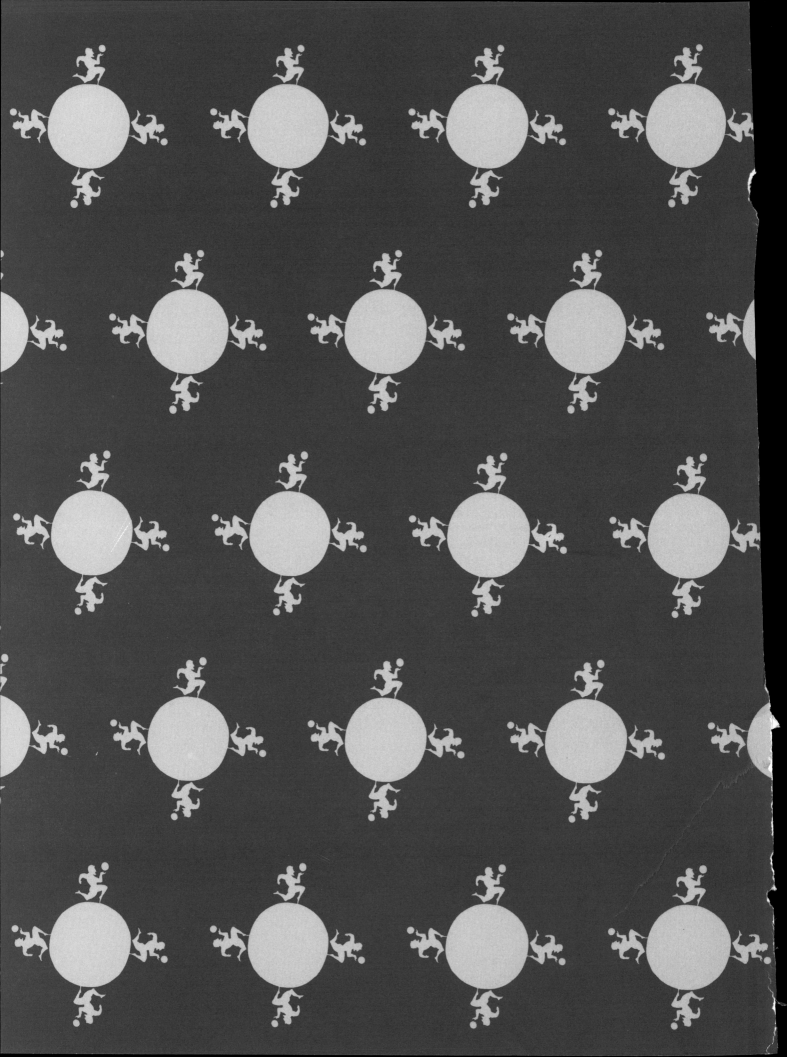